MW01581961

abdobooks.com

Published by Magic Wagon, a division of ABDO, PO Box 398166, Minneapolis, Minnesota 55439. Copyright © 2021 by Abdo Consulting Group, Inc. International copyrights reserved in all countries. No part of this book may be reproduced in any form without written permission from the publisher. Claw™ is a trademark and logo of Magic Wagon.

Printed in the United States of America, North Mankato, Minnesota.
082020
012021

Written by Bailey J. Russell
Illustrated by Neil Evans
Edited by Tamara L. Britton
Art Direction by Victoria Bates

Library of Congress Control Number: 2020930094

Publisher's Cataloging-in-Publication Data

Names: Russell, Bailey J., author. | Evans, Neil, illustrator.
Title: The seers / by Bailey J. Russell ; illustrated by Neil Evans.
Description: Minneapolis, Minnesota : Magic Wagon, 2021. | Series: The haunting of Hawthorne Harbor; book 1
Summary: On the first day of Mary's junior year she sees people who others say are not really there. From three new students, she learns that she—and they—can see ghosts. And why. But who are these new kids and what are they doing in Hawthorne Harbor?
Identifiers: ISBN 9781532138362 (lib. bdg.) | ISBN 9781532139086 (ebook) | ISBN 9781532139444 (Read-to-Me ebook)
Subjects: LCSH: High school students--Juvenile fiction. | Ghosts--Juvenile fiction. | First day of school--Juvenile fiction. | Extrasensory perception--Juvenile fiction. | Supernatural--Juvenile fiction. | Mystery and detective stories--Juvenile fiction.
Classification: DDC [FIC]--dc23

Table of CONTENTS

CHAPTER ONE	4
CHAPTER TWO	15
CHAPTER THREE	26
CHAPTER FOUR	37
CHAPTER FIVE	48
CHAPTER SIX	58
CHAPTER SEVEN	69
CHAPTER EIGHT	79
CHAPTER NINE	90
CHAPTER TEN	101

Chapter ONE

Of course, Mary Paine knew the story of the school fire. Everyone in Hawthorne Harbor knew about the tragedy. But few could remember the names.

Most of the families of the dead children had moved away after it happened. Hawthorne Harbor had built a new high school about a hundred feet from the old one. A forest of alders and blackberry vines had grown up around the charred ruins of the original school.

Mary wasn't thinking about the Fire on the first day of her junior year at Hawthorne Harbor High. As she waited for first-period English to start, she smoothed her ponytail. She touched the top of her head, smoothing the rooster tails of brown hair that stuck up.

A few kids were already in class, filling the desks from the back of the room to the front. Mary sat in the middle and watched the clock tick toward 7:45 a.m. It was too early to be awake and too hot for summer to be over. The air-conditioning didn't seem to be working and sweat slicked the backs of her knees and the crooks of her elbows.

She wanted to lay her cheek against the cool surface of her desk, but that might look weird. The last thing Mary wanted was to be weird on the first day of school. They were already talking about her, she knew. Poor Mary.

Two boys came into the classroom. One she knew. James Carter entered the room like a storm cloud. He was basically one big scowl with a sloppy undercut. Mary had told her friend Chloe to slap her if she ever started to frown that much. Chloe had said she would.

James almost stopped at Mary's desk. She could feel him slow down. But he kept walking to the back of the classroom and sat down with a loud huff. James took up more space in the world than everybody else. This had annoyed Mary when they were friends. She kind of missed it now. She didn't look back.

The other boy was interesting. Chloe, whose mom worked at the school, had called Mary last week to tell her that there would be some new kids that year. Not new kid, but kids. Plural. Then Chloe's voice had gone all squealy. Mary had to hold the phone away from her ear, so she might have missed some of the details, but this boy had to be one of them.

The new boy looked around like he wasn't sure he was in the right class. He had thick, black hair that almost covered his ears and dark skin. He smiled as he walked past Mary's desk, and she flushed. He took the seat right behind her. Mary wanted to turn around and look at him, but she didn't.

Then she felt a tap on her shoulder. She turned in her chair. His dark brown eyes were framed by long eyelashes. "Hi. I'm Daniel Vasquez. Dan. Is this English?"

"Yeah", she managed to reply. "Mrs. Polly's A.P. English. She's great."

"Thanks. This place is a maze. I walked through the cafeteria three times before I found this room. I have no idea how Tom and Abby are managing." Daniel grinned. Mary laughed and nodded along like she understood. With two new guys, Chloe would be unbearable. She turned around and went back to staring at the clock.

Tap, tap. Mary looked back over her

shoulder, hoping the position didn't give her a double chin. "Yeah?"

"You didn't tell me your name. If you don't tell me, I'll just have to keep thinking of you as the girl with the pretty hair."

Mary blushed and muttered, "Mary," then turned back around. She tried to place his accent. It was slight, but she could tell right away that he wasn't from Hawthorne Harbor.

Glancing at the still-empty door, Mary quickly took out her phone. *Dibs.* She pressed send then waited, grinning. *You found one? Hot???* Chloe always responded in seconds. Mary pictured Chloe hiding her phone under her desk, texting by feel, her eyes at the front like the perfect student.

Mary was about to text back when she had the sudden feeling of being outside of herself, watching some other Mary smile and text about boys. Hot tears squeezed her throat and she put her phone away. Every time she smiled or laughed, it hurt.

Mary didn't just miss her brother. She missed him the way she imagined a bird would miss its wings or a star would miss the sky. It was an empty, aching pain. She didn't even know who she was anymore, living in a world without him.

When the teacher walked in, Mary was trying not to cry. She got out her notebook and pen and wrote the date on the top right-hand corner of the first page. She blinked down at the lined paper, breathing in deeply through her nose and out through her mouth just like the counselor at the hospital had showed her. When Mary looked up, the teacher was not Mrs. Polly.

Her stomach dropped. Had she spaced on what room she was in? Or maybe Mrs. Polly was sick and they had a sub. Mary turned to see if anyone else looked surprised. James was chewing on his pencil like a rodent, his feet propped up on the empty chair in front of him. The other kids were either talking or just staring off into space. Daniel raised his eyebrows at her. Mary shrugged and turned back around.

"Hello class. I'm Mr. Benson," the teacher said. "And this is the first day of the rest of your life." Mr. Benson had thinning brown hair and looked to be in his late forties. He wore a brown suit that must have been hot. His glasses were thick-rimmed and black, like the kind hipsters wore. Mary wondered if her classmates would make fun of him or applaud his style.

Mr. Benson held up a book. "William Blake. I trust you've all done your reading?" Mary glanced around at the class again. No one had a book out. No one even seemed

to be paying much attention. Mr. Benson opened his book. "Today we'll be discussing 'The Tyger' along with some of Blake's other poems from the *Songs of Experience* and *Songs of Innocence* cycles. Who would like to read it aloud?"

Mary ducked her head.

"All right, I see we lack inspiration today," Mr. Benson said. "Well, we wouldn't want a half-hearted attempt at Blake. I'll read this one, though I expect volunteers for the next." He cleared his throat, made a sweeping gesture with his hand, and began:

> "Tyger Tyger, burning bright,
> In the forests of the night;
> What immortal hand or eye,
> Could frame thy fearful symmetry?"

Mr. Benson's deep voice filled the room.

He had adopted a British accent for the poem and sounded like someone performing Shakespeare. He paused. "Anyone notice the meter? The use of alliteration? The divine imagery? There should be raised hands when I'm finished." He continued:

> "In what distant deeps or skies.
> Burnt the fire of thine eyes?
> On what wings dare he aspire?
> What the hand, dare seize the fire?"

When Mr. Benson came to the word *fire*, Mary saw him flinch. He paused and wiped his hand across his brow. He was really sweating in that heavy suit. "Excuse me," he said, then repeated the last line. "What the hand, dare seize the fire?"

He spoke slower, the dramatic flair gone from his voice. Then he dropped his book. He didn't look very good. His face was red and he was blinking a lot. Mary wondered if he was having a heart attack or something. Should she go see if he was okay? No one else stood up to help, and Mary wasn't sure what to do. She didn't want to embarrass herself, or the teacher, if nothing was wrong.

While she sat frozen, still deciding how to act, Mr. Benson's legs burst into flames.

Chapter Two

Mary couldn't believe what she was seeing. The flames, as they snaked up from the teacher's leather shoes, were almost colorless under the florescent lights. They covered his legs, curled around his waist, and engulfed his whole form in translucent ribbons of fire.

His suit began to burn away, revealing patches of red, cracking skin. Within the writhing column of orange and blue flames, Mary saw Mr. Benson put his hands over his face. The backs of his hands started to blister and blacken. The air smelled like burnt hair.

It was his scream that brought Mary back to her body. She stood up, knocking over her desk. Her own scream caught at the base of her throat, and she couldn't breathe. *Water,* she thought. *We need water. And fire trucks.*

But before Mary could do anything useful, like grab the fire extinguisher that was bolted to the wall by the door, or call 911, the teacher vanished.

He didn't burn up. He simply disappeared. Everything was gone: the rushing sound of the flames, the horrible smell. His ragged screams were gone, too, though Mary could still hear his voice echoing in her ears like the ringing after a concert. Her whole body was shaking.

"Where . . . ?" She swallowed, looking wildly around the room. "The teacher, where . . . where did he go?" In the back of the room, James stood up too, dropping his pencil.

"Mary? Mare? You okay?"

The room was silent for a long moment. Mary could hear James's pencil rolling under a desk.

Then someone laughed. It was a nervous laughter, the kind that might bubble up at a funeral. The kind that can't be helped. Soon half the class was laughing, and the other half was whispering. Mary heard "nervous breakdown" and "crazy." She heard her brother's name.

Tears filled Mary's eyes. She ran from the room, pushing past Mrs. Polly, who was walking through the door. Just before she ran, however, Mary had looked at Daniel.

The new boy hadn't been laughing or whispering like the others. His eyes were closed and he was gripping the edge of his desk, like he was trying to hold himself in place. Like he might float away if he let go.

Mary ran to the girl's bathroom and locked herself in the nearest stall. Though the walls had been wiped clean of most of last year's writing, there were still a few words carved into the smooth surface. *Have a nice day!* stood out in jagged letters on the back of the door, just below a smiley face.

Mary sat on the back of the toilet, with her feet on the seat. She held her hands out in front of her face. They were shaking, and blotchy, like the blood had been squeezed out of them. They looked like a stranger's hands.

Mary remembered the teacher's hands covering his face and how the flames had rippled across them. But it couldn't have been real. A man could not just burn up while a room full of students ignored it. Mary kept looking at her hands because when she closed her eyes she could see Mr. Benson's, covered with charred blisters.

The bathroom door opened. Mary held her breath, clasping her shaking hands over her chest. She stared at the word *nice*, willing the person to leave. The person paused outside

Mary's stall. The shoes were familiar.

"Mary?"

It was James. Mary did not want to see James right now. If she saw James, a hole would open in the center of her lungs and they would both fall in. "Mare? You can't hide in the bathroom. Only crazy people hide in bathrooms."

"Go. Away." Each word brought Mary closer to tears. Her throat ached. She clenched her hands tighter to her rib cage, like she was trying to hold something in.

"I can crawl under. I'm still—what did you used to call me? Skinny as a toothpick?"

Mary let out a ragged sigh. She stepped down from the toilet and opened the door. As soon as she walked out of the stall, James wrapped her in a hug. She stiffened and turned her face away from his chest.

He was skinny. Mary could feel the outline

of his ribs pressed against her, the bones of his arms on her back. James was tall, too, with a large nose and a face full of angles. His mother used to say that he would grow into his face, though she didn't live to see it.

But in class earlier, Mary had noticed that his face had changed over the summer. Matured. The awkward angles had developed into a strong jaw and sharp cheekbones. She was starting to see the adult he would one day become, and it left her with a sense of vertigo at how quickly the world was speeding forward.

James set his chin on top of her head. "Mary. Are you okay? I wanted to come see you after . . ." He trailed off, not saying the words.

So Mary said them for him: "After Paul died? You wanted to see me then?" She pushed him away. "You're a jerk."

"You're just mad." His voice was pleading, and he reached out his hand to touch her shoulder. "I was mad too, when my mom died."

She brushed him away, then folded her arms across her chest. "We're not part of some club now," she said. Mary had never really wanted to hurt James before. She did now. "You don't get to understand me just because your mom's dead."

Mary didn't meet James's eyes but looked over his shoulder to the row of mirrors above the sinks. Her face was washed-out and wild: red, puffy eyes, lips the color of sand. She closed her eyes, then looked down at the fraying cuffs of James's jeans. His dirty shoes. Without his mom to make him go school shopping, he was still wearing his old, scuffed Chucks.

James's mother had died about eight

months earlier. Lung cancer. It was crazy fast. They didn't even know she was sick, and then she had only a few weeks left. Weeks are nothing. Weeks are a puff of air.

Sherry Carter was the first person Mary had really known who had died. Mary thought losing James's mom was the worst thing that could happen. She felt James's grief when she sat next to him in class. It radiated from his skin like a sunburn. She felt it when they went to his house after school and his dad looked fragile somehow.

Back then, Mary had thought she understood James, and that they were grieving together. She didn't realize that James was experiencing a degree of pain she didn't even know could exist at the time.

Mary, James, and Chloe always used to hang out at James's house. One of Chloe's revolving boyfriends sometimes made a fourth. But it was usually just the three of them. More specifically, it was Mary and James, and then Chloe. She had joined them in seventh grade, when her parents divorced and Chloe's mom moved to Hawthorne Harbor.

Mary and James had been friends since preschool, when Mary held James's hand and James didn't push her down or spit in her hair. Later, he did push her and spit in her hair. But by then they were already friends and Mary had learned how to spit back.

James's parents' basement had been converted into a game room. It had a huge flat-screen TV, an Xbox One, and a Nintendo Switch. A fridge was kept stocked with Coke for James, root beer for Mary, and sparkling water for Chloe.

After James's mom died, Chloe stopped coming over as much. James was too moody, too hard to be around. But Mary still did homework at James's kitchen table. She ignored the awkward silences when she knew James was thinking about his mom. She ignored the scowls and the temper he didn't used to have.

Chapter THREE

One afternoon, right at the beginning of summer, Mary and James had been watching one of their favorite movies. The curtains were drawn against the sun, and the only light in the room came from the flickering TV.

James had cranked the AC so high that Mary had goose bumps on her bare arms. It was beautiful outside: the harbor shining, the trees still clinging to the new green of spring. The kind of day that people in the Pacific Northwest couldn't help but savor.

Chloe's dad was visiting and had taken her and her sister sailing. Chloe had just texted Mary a picture of herself in a purple life jacket and oversized sunglasses. Her blond hair was pushed back with a headband and hung loose around her shoulders. *U should B here.* Mary didn't reply, but she felt a tinge of guilt, like she was wasting a beautiful day.

But all Mary wanted that afternoon was to sit with her friend in the dark and wait for his grief to evaporate. So when James had tried to kiss her, Mary was shocked.

At first, Mary was too surprised to move. Then, she had pushed him away. "James!" Mary tried to keep her voice quiet because James's dad was upstairs. "What the heck?"

James covered his face with his hands. He said something that Mary couldn't quite hear. She leaned closer. "What?" Even though she was freaked out, she still felt like she needed to protect him. From his grief, perhaps. From himself. She touched his hands. "It's okay. We're okay."

He dropped his hands and looked at her,

looked past her. "Leave," he said, his voice low and harsh—like a stranger's voice. Like a slap. "Just go!"

She left him in the dark basement in the glow of the TV. But she texted him later, telling him again that it was okay. They were okay. He didn't text back.

All summer, he was gone. He didn't return her calls or texts. Wouldn't answer the door when she knocked. His dad said that he just needed some space, but what Mary heard was *James hates you. James isn't coming back.* Then when Mary's life fell apart, James was still gone. She hated him for it. And they were officially not okay.

Now, in the girls' bathroom, Mary faced James. She felt like she was standing on one of those moving walkways in an airport. Even though she hadn't moved, the distance between her and her old best friend was growing wider and deeper with every second. She wanted it that way.

"I know how you feel." James spoke slowly, like he was talking to a child. "I know the world is messed up. I know you hate everything." Then softer, "I know you hate me."

Mary shook her head, finally letting the tears spill down her face. "You don't know anything. Your mom didn't kill herself."

James sucked in his breath. "Mare, Paul didn't... it was a car accident. He didn't want to die."

"Doesn't matter." Mary shook her head again and again, like she was telling the world *no*. *No* to Paul's death. *No* to her brother's car wrapped around a tree. *No* to his unrecognizable face, his missing arm. *No* to the week he spent on life support.

"It doesn't matter," she said, and she walked past James.

"Wait."

Mary didn't turn around, but she hesitated, her hand on the bathroom door.

"In the classroom, what happened? You really freaked out. That wasn't just about Paul..."

"It was nothing." Mary didn't have a tissue, so she rubbed her nose with the back of her hand, then wiped the snot on her jeans.

"You looked like you saw something."

"It was nothing," she repeated.

"It's just, I thought I saw—"

But Mary was already walking away, the heavy door closing over James's words.

Mary went to her other morning classes, sat in the back, and hardly listened to the teachers. It was like the movie of her life had paused when she ran out of first period, and she was waiting for someone to hit play again.

When she got to the cafeteria for lunch,

she scanned the crowd for Chloe but didn't see her. James sat at an empty table, looking at his phone. It was strange to think that he had no other friends. Remove Mary from James's world, and he was alone. He didn't even try. He just sat by himself with a slice of cheese pizza and a bottle of Coke.

Mary was so busy not paying attention to James that she didn't see the man in the gray coveralls until he brushed past her. She could smell something wafting off the man—motor oil or grease. The man looked back at her, just for a moment. He was wearing dark welding goggles and was holding something in his hands. A big oilcan? Air tank? She wasn't sure. Mary kept walking.

A moment later she found Chloe sitting alone at a table that was covered with backpacks and littered with flyers for the Lock-In on Friday.

"What...?" Mary began, gesturing towards the backpacks.

Chloe cut her off. "I found them!" Her smile was maniacal. "These are their bags. They're sitting with us!" Chloe wore a short blue dress and silver leggings. Her hair was pulled back in a tight bun like a ballerina's, and silver hoops dangled from her ears. Chloe always said she had a fat face, but Mary thought she was beautiful.

"You found who?"

"Come on, Mary." Chloe rolled her eyes, giving her an *I can't believe I even have to explain this to you* look. I texted you!"

Mary hadn't checked her phone since first period. "I give up."

"The new kids! They're in line right now. I'm watching their bags."

"Why are they sitting with us?" Mary had been looking forward to lunch because Chloe would do all the talking and Mary could eat in peace. She knew Chloe wouldn't ask her about her freak-out in English or bring up her brother. Chloe's conversations were like cotton candy—light, fluffy, nothing. Sometimes Mary was grateful for that.

"Because I asked. And they said yes!" Chloe took out her Tupperware of salad, an even smaller Tupperware of balsamic vinaigrette, and a fork. She stabbed a cherry tomato. "You met one already, right?" She smirked. "Dibs?"

Mary blushed and took a large bite of sandwich so she didn't have to answer. That was, of course, the moment that Daniel and the two other new kids sat down.

"Hey—Mary, right?" Daniel set his tray next to her. She nodded, her mouth too full to say anything. Now that she could see him without twisting her neck, he didn't look quite how she remembered. His nose was slightly crooked and he had a little scar on his chin. His eyes were just as dark, though, and she tried not to stare. She looked down at her sandwich.

She waited for him to ask her about English class and why she had run out of the room like a crazy person. But he didn't. Instead, he motioned to the two strangers who sat across the table, next to Chloe. "Have you met Tom and Abby?"

She swallowed the bite of sandwich then answered, "No, not yet. I'm Mary."

Tom had light brown hair—almost red—and it stuck up messily. He had probably styled it that way. His eyes were somehow the same color as his hair. A smile tugged at the corners of his mouth. "Sure. We've heard all about you."

Mary tried not to scowl. She tried so hard that she thought there might be a vein popping out on her forehead, just above her left eyebrow. There were so many things to choose from—had they heard all about her dead brother or all about the desk she knocked over like a freak?

Chapter FOUR

Abby cut in. "Chloe told us that you like movies." Abby was gorgeous, with long, red hair and eyes the blue-green color of a mountain lake.

"Yeah. I mean, most people like movies."

"But you'd know the best place to go see a movie, right? In town?" Abby's tray was heaping with two large slices of pizza, a mound of Tater Tots, three cookies, and a chocolate milk. Mary didn't even know they'd give you more than one cookie. She'd never asked.

"Well, there's really only one place—the Opal. It's an old theater down on Main. Kinda small, but really cool."

Chloe nodded. "There's a film festival this

week. You guys should go. The Opal has great popcorn."

Daniel looked at Mary. "You want to?"

"What?" Oh, great, Mary. Great.

"We could go see a movie. If you want . . ." Before she could answer, he added, "All of us, I mean."

"I'm busy tonight," Mary said, at the crust of her sandwich.

"What about tomorrow?" Chloe said, kicking Mary under the table. "I'm having dinner with my dad—but Mary's free. And isn't there a movie you wanted to see, Mare?"

Mary tried to glare at Chloe while still smiling at the others. She probably looked ill. "Yeah . . . *The Gallery*. But it's in French. And black-and-white. Real artsy."

"Sounds good," Abby said. "I speak a little French. *Voulez-vous coucher avec moi?*"

"Singing along to the *Moulin Rouge!*

sound track in the shower does not count as 'speaking a little French,'" Tom said. Abby rolled her eyes then took a big bite of pizza.

"Okay." Mary attempted a more successful smile. "I think it starts at eight—do you need directions?"

Tom was already typing something into his phone. "Google Maps. It's the Age of Miracles!"

Abby flicked Tom in the temple with one of her long fingers. "What he means to say is that we'll meet you there."

"Are you two a couple?" Mary asked Tom and Abby before she could stop herself. She always did that when she was nervous—blurted out personal questions like she was a reporter or something. It was probably the reason she and Chloe had become such good friends. Chloe loved to talk about herself.

"Mary!" Chloe groaned in exactly the same

tone she used when her mom did something embarrassing, like leave the house in her bathrobe to get the mail. The other three laughed.

"She's my sister," Tom offered, still smiling. "We weren't properly introduced. Thomas and Abigail Moore, at your service."

"They're twins," Daniel said.

"Yeah," Tom said, "but I got all the dashing good looks." This earned a snort from Abby.

"Wait," Chloe said through a bite of salad, pointing her fork at Daniel. "How do you know them? Did you meet at some *So! You've just moved to the most boring town in the world!* convention before school started?"

"Yeah," Mary asked. "Why'd you guys move here?"

Just then a scream cut through the lunchroom chatter and everyone went silent. It came from the lunch line. Mary stood up, trying to see over a mob of students. She could just barely make out a girl holding her hands to her head. It was Patricia Wilson, who had long, blond hair that hung down to her waist. Or, used to: a huge chunk of her hair was now smoldering around her ears.

"Wow," Mary blurted at the same time Tom said, "Look at that." Chloe put down her fork, her mouth hanging open.

"It was Liam," someone called out. Mary realized there was a boy beneath the mob of students. A few people were holding his arms others had his legs.

The new vice principal, Mr. Flynn, pushed his way through the crowd. Mr. Flynn looked like an actor playing a washed-up football star. He had thinning blond hair and a bit of a gut, but his shoulders were broad enough to still be intimidating. He lifted Liam off the ground and marched him through the

lunchroom. Mary saw Liam drop a lighter and kick it across the room.

Some girls helped Patty, holding on to her arms as they walked her to the nurse's office. When she passed their table, Mary could see that the skin along Patty's neck was red and blistered and the collar of her shirt was burned.

As Patty left the lunchroom, the stunned silence began to fill with whispers. The school now had something even bigger to talk about than Mary's dead brother or her freak-out that morning.

Mary's phone buzzed. She had a new text. James: *What happened?* James was on the other side of the room and probably hadn't been able to see Patty's neck or Liam being dragged away. She considered writing back but put her phone away instead.

"Wowzers," Abby spoke up. "I can't imagine

how that must have hurt."

"Did you see her neck?" Tom added. "Brutal. She'll probably have scars."

"I'd kill Liam if I were her," Chloe said. "I'd just rip his face right off. What a psycho."

Mary set down her sandwich. Off to the side of the room, just beyond the crowd, Mary noticed that same construction worker with the goggles. He was smiling.

"You know who that is, right?" Chloe asked.

"The construction guy?" Mary responded.

"Who? No, Mr. Flynn." She paused, recovering her fork from where she put it on the table and wiping it off with a napkin. "He's Principal Hawthorne's grandson." While everyone else in the lunchroom was still talking about Patty's burned hair, Chloe somehow was eating.

Mary took another look at the man in the goggles. Chloe had seen him, right?

"Hawthorne...like in Hawthorne Harbor?" Daniel asked.

The others gave Chloe their full attention. "You've heard about the Fire, right?" They nodded.

"Well, Principal Hawthorne died in that fire. He was trying to save one of the students—his nephew, I think—and the ceiling fell. They were both crushed."

"That sucks," Tom said, stealing one of his sister's Tater Tots before she could swat his hand away. Dan took one of her cookies.

"Knock it off." Abby moved her tray away from the two boys and put her arms protectively around it. "But I thought Hawthorne Harbor was named after the water."

The crystal-clear harbor was surrounded by high, crumbling bluffs that loomed above it. It was one of Hawthorne Harbor's most photographed features. Quaint Victorian houses perched on the edge of the bluffs, resembling birds about to take flight.

"No," Mary spoke up. "A lot of people think that. It's actually named after the Hawth— one of the founding families." Mary only knew that because of the local history class they all had to take in middle school. She thought using the phrase "founding families" might make her sound smart.

Chloe nodded. "After the Fire, most of the Hawthorne family moved away. But my mom told me that Mr. Flynn had an aunt or someone who just died and left him a house. So he's back."

"Spooky, right?" Tom's eyes were practically sparkling. "He works at the school and the first day, there's a fire. Coincidence?" He suddenly reminded Mary of a leprechaun, with his reddish hair and the way he kept rubbing his hands together like he was plotting something. She wondered whether he even realized he was doing it.

Mary shook her head. "It was just a nut job with a lighter." She glanced back at the weird construction worker, but he was gone.

chapter FIVE

After school, Mary headed over to the Harbor Breeze Retirement Plaza. Mary had missed the last three weeks since Paul died. Putting on her green shirt with the Harbor Breeze sailboat logo felt good. Almost normal. The receptionist looked up from her computer as Mary walked in the door. "Mary! Did you see the fire at school?"

Mary stopped and stared at Corinne. "The fire?" She pictured Mr. Benson's legs burning. She still hadn't mentioned the teacher—her hallucination— to anyone.

Corinne pushed her reading glasses onto the top of her head. They always tangled in her hair, pulling strands out of her already messy bun. "I heard some girl's hair was on fire. How terrible! Were you there?"

"Yeah. It was pretty bad. I guess Liam Russell was playing with a lighter in the lunch line, and it caught on Patricia Wilson's hair."

Corinne shook her head. She put her reading glasses back on her nose, pulling more hair loose, and went back to typing.

Harbor Breeze Retirement Plaza wasn't the only old folks home in Hawthorne Harbor, but it was the nicest. From the front steps there was a great view of the water, and on a rare clear day you could see the mountains rising up in the distance.

Mary and Chloe both started volunteering at Harbor Breeze at the same time, but Chloe quit after the first day. Chloe had just said, "Old people stress me out," and the matter was closed.

But Mary kept going back, and not just because it would look good on her college applications. She just felt like a better person when she was there. Gone was the sarcastic, moody Mary. She was replaced by a smiling, respectful teenage girl who could produce small talk for hours.

Sure, some of the residents gave her the creeps, like the one old man with the glass eye. But most of the people were really nice, like grandparents. Her own grandparents lived in Arizona, so she hardly ever saw them.

If Mary had to get old, she wouldn't mind living there. There were always plates of cookies sitting out and free coffee. Mary emptied four creamers and three packets of sugar into a green Harbor Breeze mug and filled it the rest of the way with weak coffee from the dispenser.

Mary helped out in the dining room sometimes, taking residents' orders. Other days she tidied the activities room. If there was nothing that needed to be done, she played cards with Eleanor McDonald. Eleanor was almost ninety and had been married four times. She always had on bright red lipstick and, even though she was in a wheelchair, wore high-heeled shoes.

Mary checked the board. Bingo had just ended, which meant Eleanor was probably still down in the activities room. She wanted to tell Eleanor about Patty's burning hair. Then, if she could stand the teasing, she would tell her about Daniel. Eleanor was always asking Mary about the boys in her life, and now she actually had a sort-of date with a tall, dark, and mysterious stranger.

The activities room was really nice—with a flat-screen TV and huge potted trees that made the place look like a resort. It always smelled like orange cleanser and coffee. Some of the residents were reading or watching the news. Eleanor was in the far corner, her wheelchair pushed up to a card table. Clara Deville was showing Eleanor pictures on an iPad. When Eleanor saw Mary, she rolled her eyes. Mary smiled.

"Hi ladies," Mary grinned at the two women. "Isn't it a beautiful day?" The weather had actually turned out a bit drizzly, but Mary tried to be optimistic.

Eleanor picked up a cup of coffee with a red slash of lipstick on the rim. "Hi, honey. We've missed you." She always spoke slowly, her voice a little shaky. "Welcome back."

Clara looked up. "I was just showing Eleanor the pictures my daughter brought me. Here's my new great-grandson." The woman held the device toward Mary. The head of a red-faced newborn took up most of the screen. Mary thought he looked like a mole.

"He's precious!" she gushed.

"Yes, well." Clara smiled. "My daughter says he takes after my late husband."

"I'm sure he does. So adorable."

Mary took a seat and told them both the news from school. Clara put her hand to her chest. "Oh dear. Her hair?"

Eleanor adjusted her glasses. "A fire at school?" Her glasses made her already large blue eyes gigantic.

"Just a small fire—an accident. No one was really hurt." Mary thought about Patty's neck. She didn't actually know how badly she was burned. It hadn't looked good.

Eleanor pointed to a woman reading a book one table over. "Honey, did you know that Jane was in the Fire?" When talking about the school fire of 1966, you didn't need to specify. It was just the Fire, capital F. Mary shook her head. But when she thought about it, she remembered hearing that Jane Owens had been a teacher.

Mary had noticed Jane's scars before but hadn't thought about them. Jane's right arm was a mass of scar tissue, from the wrist to where her floral shirtsleeve reached her elbow. There was also some scarring up her neck, where the flames had probably licked the right side of her face. Mary hoped that Patty's neck would heal better than Jane's had.

Jane turned toward them. Mary knew she had been caught staring at Jane's scarred arm, so she said, "I love your bracelet," nodding at the white charm bracelet circling the old woman's wrist.

"Oh, this." Jane smiled, touching the bracelet with her other hand. "A gift from my grandmother."

"It's lovely!" Mary said. And it really was—

tiny, delicate figures carved from what looked like ivory. "Where did your grandmother get it?" Mary had learned early on that the residents loved to talk about their family history.

Jane frowned momentarily, and Mary hoped she hadn't unearthed a bad memory. Once Mary had asked a female resident about her beloved dog and the woman had started sobbing. Mary always tried to keep conversations light and cheerful after that.

Jane's brow cleared. "My grandfather gave it to her. He was a whaler in Alaska. These are made from . . . whalebone."

"Wow!" Mary had a flash of a young man dressed in a fur-lined coat, standing on the deck of a whaling boat. "He must have led a fascinating life," she said.

History was Mary's favorite subject. That was another reason why she loved coming to

Harbor Breeze. Talking to some of the people was better than watching documentaries or reading memoirs. They had lived through history and had been a part of it.

"Yes. He was a special man." Jane picked up her book and turned away. Mary wanted to keep talking, to ask her more about her grandfather and Alaska, but she didn't. Instead, she told Eleanor and Clara about her upcoming date and then spent the next hour losing at cards.

chapter SIX

Mary had been looking forward to the Junior/Senior Lock-In since Paul was a freshman and came home talking about it. On the first Friday night of every school year, the oldest students spent the night at school. They ate pizza and candy, drank pop, and slept in the lunchroom in sleeping bags. The tradition had been going on for as long as Mary could remember.

Of course, the students weren't left entirely to their own devices. A few chaperones checked in on them every now and again from another wing of the school. But for the most part the students were left alone, and they looked forward to it for years.

When Paul was a junior, Mary had asked

for every detail. He told her she would have to wait her turn. What Mary really wanted to know was what the senior prank had been. She had heard that the seniors waited until everyone was asleep and then started shooting everyone with paintballs. Like, in the face and everything. Mary heard that a girl almost lost an eye.

Paul had just shaken his head and smiled.

Mary pressed on. "So was it paintball guns? Did they have night vision goggles? Did they chase you through the classrooms?"

"Do you really think the school would let the seniors bring guns to school? Even fake guns?" Paul had said.

But that wasn't a *no*. And the chaperones let the seniors get away with almost anything during the Lock-In. Everyone knew that.

When Paul was a senior, and she was a sophomore, Mary gave him constant prank suggestions: You could dress up like zombies and have fake brains to eat. You could wake the juniors up in the middle of the night with water guns. You could steal their bags and put them in the swimming pool.

Paul had laughed at all of her ideas. She never did learn exactly what Paul's class ended up doing. But she knew it involved a lot of shaving cream, because he came home from the store with the back of his car full of those aerosol cans.

Last year's juniors were now seniors, and they had started a countdown to the Lock-In. They put up a huge sign that hung in the juniors' locker hallway. On Wednesday, it said THREE DAYS.

"The seniors are too stupid to think of their own prank," Chloe said, taking her Algebra textbook out of her locker. Mary was glad that her first class was not math. She needed to be awake for a few more hours before the math part of her brain came to life.

"Yeah. I bet they'll just cover us in shaving cream like Paul's class."

"Is that what they did? That's pretty lame." Chloe was one of the few people who would still talk about Paul like he was a normal person and not some perfect saint now that he was dead.

"I don't think that's all they did . . . I bet it was really freaky at the time. Maybe they brought in black lights that made everyone look like zombies." Mary wasn't quite over her zombie phase.

"Um . . . still pretty lame. When we're seniors our prank is going to give the juniors PTSD, and they'll probably still be wetting their beds in college."

"That's our Chloe, always aiming for the stars."

"Yes indeedy."

Mary and Chloe headed in different directions for first period. As Mary walked down the hall, Mr. Flynn appeared beside her. "Miss Paine?"

"Oh, hi, Mr. Flynn. I'm not late for class, am I?"

"No, no. I just wanted to have a quick chat with you. I've already told your teacher." Mr. Flynn was more than six feet tall and towered over Mary. He was wearing a button-down shirt with the sleeves rolled up, exposing his hairy forearms.

"Um, okay." She followed him to his office, watching his broad back as they walked.

Mary wondered why the old vice principal, Mrs. Bagley, had resigned. She was a chubby, short woman who looked like an owl, with round wire-frame glasses and gray hair. Some students called her the Bag Lady, but Mary never did. After Paul died, Mrs. Bagley had sent Mary's family a card with a picture of a sad puppy wearing a blue bow. Mary wasn't sure how the sad puppy was supposed to make her feel better about her dead brother, but she supposed it was the thought that counted.

Mr. Flynn's office smelled like incense, which surprised Mary. It was fairly unpleasant—a cloying, cinnamony kind of scent. She sneezed.

"Have a seat." Mr. Flynn motioned to the chair across from him. "First, I want to say how sorry I was to hear about your brother. I'm sure he was a wonderful young man. All of the teachers spoke highly of him."

"Thanks," Mary said. She never knew what to say when people told her they were sorry. Was she thankful that Mr. Flynn had made her think about her dead brother during a school day? She swallowed and looked around the room.

On the wall was a black-and-white picture of the old school, taken almost a century earlier. A crowd of people gathered around the large, brick building. The picture focused on a pair of boys walking down the front stairs. They were smiling and wearing those short pants and tall socks that you see on kids in old-timey movies.

"You know I lost someone myself when I was about your age," Mr. Flynn said.

"Your grandfather?" Mary asked, still looking at the photograph.

Mr. Flynn startled. "My grandfather? Do you mean Principal Hawthorne?"

She nodded.

"I suppose, though I wasn't talking about him. I wasn't even born yet when the Fire happened. I'm only forty-three," he chuckled.

"Oh." Only? Mary couldn't imagine being in her forties.

"No worries. I was actually talking about my sister. She was hit by a car when she was six years old. Died instantly. I was sixteen."

"I'm sorry."

"Thanks." He paused, looking Mary right in the eye. She didn't usually make eye contact with teachers or other authority figures, and it was a little unsettling, like maybe he could read her mind.

"After my sister died, I acted out—especially at school. I stopped doing my homework, skipped class, and lied to my teachers. I didn't know how to handle it until I started talking to someone."

Mary knew where this was going. Mr. Flynn was going to bring up her freak-out yesterday and recommend that she see the school counselor. Or maybe a real shrink? "I already saw a grief counselor," she said. "At the hospital."

"That's a good start. And you know that the school counselor is available whenever you want. If you need to take a break from class and drop by Ms. Rye's office, by all means do so. But that wasn't exactly what I meant. Do you have any close friends? Someone you can talk to?"

"Yeah. I have some great friends." Mary meant Chloe. But then she thought of James. In third grade, she had her tonsils removed, and James had ridden his bike over to her house with a pint of ice cream. It had melted all over the inside of his backpack, and Mary couldn't even eat it because the doctors said she couldn't have dairy for two weeks.

"If you ever feel . . . out of control . . . like yesterday, please know that there are a lot of people you can ask for help. And my door is always open." It was open then. The school must have a rule about male employees and female students. But Mr. Flynn did have a nice smile, like he actually wanted to help.

"Thanks, Mr. Flynn. I'll keep that in mind." Mary stood up to leave.

"And Miss Paine," he added as she was walking toward the door, "have fun at the Lock-In."

Chapter SEVEN

As Mary walked to first period, she lifted her arm to her nose to see whether she still smelled like Mr. Flynn's incense. No, thank God. She took slow, careful footsteps across the linoleum floor. It was never good to show up late for class. The last thing she wanted was to walk in that door and face everyone's stares and whispers.

When she reached the door, Mary paused. She checked her phone—no new messages. She ran her fingers through her hair and reapplied her lip gloss. After retying her shoes and making sure her backpack was zipped, she finally reached for the door.

Before she opened it, she saw movement in the corner of her eye. Turning her head,

Mary saw the man in the gray coveralls about ten feet away. He was leaning against the wall next to a fire alarm. He was still wearing those dark goggles and seemed to be watching her. That same smell filled the air—gasoline, kerosene—something flammable.

"Hello?" Mary said. Why was he wearing those weird clothes? He looked like he belonged in one of those steampunk video games her brother used to play. The way the man was watching her felt too familiar, too intimate. "Excuse me, I have to go to class," she said, pushing open the door.

As she entered the room, she felt a sudden heat on her back and could smell something burning. But when she looked back, the hallway was empty. As she took her seat, Mary brushed a hand across her back. The rivets on her jeans were hot to the touch.

She had never been happier to hear the

final bell than she was that afternoon.

That evening, Mary got to the Opal a little early. She waited outside the theater for Daniel and his friends. She fiddled with her phone to look like she wasn't being stood up.

There was a chill to the air, and Mary didn't have a coat. The salty wind blew hard off the harbor and made her shiver. She wished Chloe were with her then she'd at least have someone to talk to.

When there were only five minutes left before the movie started, Mary decided to buy her ticket and went inside. She hated missing the previews.

"One for *The Gallery*." She slid a twenty under the glass window. "My friends are late."

"Of course," the woman replied, sliding her change and the ticket back. Mary didn't think the woman believed her.

Stepping into the Opal was like going back

in time. The carpeting was a rich red and the concession counter was polished wood. The faded, ancient wallpaper was covered with movie posters: those showing old Hitchcock movies, westerns, and Marilyn Monroe's playful wink were hung alongside others featuring the latest blockbusters.

The theater was almost empty. That was what Mary loved about film festivals—there were always a few movies that no one really wanted to see and then you could have the whole place to yourself. An older couple sat near the front and a few college-age guys sat in the back. The guys were probably taking a film class and got credit for turning in a ticket stub.

There was one other person, a young woman sitting right in the middle of the room. That was where Mary liked to sit: exactly in the heart of the theater, where the screen was as huge as it could be without having to tilt your head up and the sound wrapped around you.

Mary sat two rows behind the woman and one seat to the right. She tried not to be annoyed that the back of the woman's head almost blocked the bottom-left corner of the screen. She put her phone on silent as soon as the previews started. She felt stupid for not getting Daniel's number.

About fifteen minutes after the movie started, Mary was surprised to see Daniel walking down the aisle. She ducked a little lower in her seat so she could watch him. With the light from the movie flickering across his face, he looked like a fake version of himself—another projection that might vanish when the lights came on.

It didn't take him long to find her. He kept his head low as he sidled up the row, as though he might be blocking someone's view in the nearly empty theater.

"Hey, sorry I'm late," Daniel said in a loud whisper. He was holding a large popcorn, and the smell of salt and butter made Mary's stomach growl.

Mary didn't ask permission before sinking her hand into the bag. "You missed the beginning," she whispered back. She wanted to be cool and aloof about the whole "date" thing, but she couldn't help herself. She was grinning.

"That's okay," he said. "I'll figure it out." He positioned the popcorn so they could share, then leaned back in his chair and put his feet up on the seat in front of him. He stared at the screen as though already absorbed in the movie, only moving to shovel popcorn into his mouth.

"Daniel?"

"Yeah?" He didn't lift his eyes from the screen.

"Where are the others?"

"You can call me Dan, if you want. Daniel's so long. Everyone shortens it eventually."

"Okay," she said, waiting for him to answer her question. But he went back to watching the movie.

"Um, Dan? Tom and Abby?"

"Oh. They couldn't make it."

The woman in the seat ahead of Mary kept turning around and looking sternly at her and Daniel every time they spoke. Mary stopped talking and tried to concentrate on the movie.

Mary was a little disappointed that the others didn't show. They were the kind of people you couldn't help but want to impress. She wondered whether they thought the movie sounded boring. It was kind of boring.

So far, the main character had just wandered around the art gallery, looking at abstract black-and-white paintings. They were some kind of abstract art, with triangles and splotches of what Mary assumed were colors, but since the movie was in black-and-white, she couldn't be sure.

Daniel spoke through a mouth full of popcorn. "Is the girl dreaming? Where is she?"

The woman turned again, glaring. This time she actually put her finger to her lips and shushed them.

Sorry, Mary mouthed back, then answered Dan. "I don't know."

"Those paintings are creepy. Do you think she's going to fall into one, like that little girl in *The Witches*?"

"I love that movie!"

The woman turned again, and Mary's face grew hot. "Dan, I think we're being too loud."

"No way. This place is empty." He munched loudly on popcorn and put his feet higher up on the seat. The seats were old, and his squeaked every time he moved.

Using her softest whisper, Mary said, "We're bothering her."

"Who?" Dan looked confused.

"Her." Mary pointed at the woman, who had put her hand to the side of her head and sighed loudly.

Dan's expression dissolved into a broad grin. "I knew it. Tom owes me fifty bucks."

Chapter EIGHT

Mary's heart dropped, and her smile turned into a scowl. Tom paid Dan to go to the movies with her? "You're here on a bet?"

She grabbed her purse and stood up. "Enjoy the movie."

The woman gave an exasperated sigh. She looked up at Mary, and in the dim light her face was pale. She was young, maybe early twenties, and her lashes were long and thick. Her eyebrows looked like they had been drawn on with permanent marker, and her lips were dark. "Please do be quiet," she said in an exaggerated whisper.

"Sorry!" Mary hissed just as Dan grabbed her wrist.

"Wait. Jeez, you're touchy. Just wait a sec."

"Let go," Mary growled. She felt raw and exposed, like a live wire.

"This isn't a dare. I mean, yeah, there was a bet involved, but—no. I just wanted to show you something." Daniel let go of her, but kept his hand raised like he was trying to calm a wild animal. He took a deep breath. "Just sit down. Please. I'll explain."

The couple at the front of the theater were now looking their way, so Mary sat, feeling flushed and foolish. That seemed to be her constant state of being lately—mortification.

"What?" Mary crossed her arms and looked back at the screen. A man had entered the art gallery, and the girl was showing him one of the ugly paintings. They were laughing about something, but Mary had missed the subtitles and didn't understand French. She wanted to know what was so funny.

Daniel leaned closer, and she stiffened.

"There's no easy way to do this. I wish there was, but there isn't. It's like a Band-Aid—you just have to rip it off. I just want you to know that you're going to be freaked out and confused at first, but it's okay. It'll get better—I promise."

Great. She was on a date with a crazy person. At least a theater was fairly public. If she screamed, someone would probably try to help.

"Okay, here goes. Look at the woman in front of us. Really look at her."

The woman turned back around. "Some of us are trying to watch the film." Her voice was jagged. While the woman was facing them, Mary looked at her—really looked, just like Daniel had asked.

When she really looked, Mary could see the light from the movie filtering through the woman's face. It was almost imperceptible:

the way the woman's skin caught the light. It reminded Mary of the paper lanterns that her parents hung in their backyard in the summer. The woman glowed, and when Mary tilted her head to the side, she could actually see the movie playing through her face. Mary gasped, then shut her eyes, tight.

"You see her. I know you see her. I guess I could've just told you at school—hey, person I just met, I think you can see ghosts. But what would you have said?" Daniel's breath was warm against her ear. "I mean, the chances of you believing me would have been exactly zero, right? Tom and Abby thought I should show you. Tom bet me fifty bucks that you weren't a Seer, but I knew you were."

Mary opened her eyes and looked at the woman. She had turned back to the movie and was touching the side of her face again. What she was touching, Mary realized, was a

bloody wound in her temple. A trickle of blood ran along her ear and down her jawline. Bits of tissue were caught in her long, dark hair. Her pale, translucent fingers kept touching the wound, then pulling back. Again and again.

"She's a ghost?" Mary whispered. Her words came out as a question, but it wasn't. She was trying to tell Daniel—tell the world, or maybe herself—that this couldn't happen. When she said the word *ghost*, the woman turned and stared at Mary, her face stricken. Her dark, glowing eyes filled with tears.

"She doesn't seem to remember most of the time." Dan's voice was lower, more serious than she had heard it so far. "She'll forget. Her kind want to forget." In a few seconds, the woman's eyes cleared and she turned back around. Her fingers grazed her temple again, then pulled away.

Mary stared at Daniel. His face was no longer cute or mysterious. He was just a stranger, and she had never felt more alone. Daniel let the silence pool around both of them until Mary felt she would drown in it. Finally, she whispered, "She's dead?"

"Shhh. She can still hear you." As Daniel said those words, the woman looked back at Mary and then vanished. "I think you scared her."

"What?" Mary had scared *her*? She stood up and looked over the back of the seat where the woman had been sitting, but it was completely empty. Mary remembered how the burning teacher had disappeared. But that had all been in her head, right? Was she hallucinating now?

"I found her on my first day in town," Daniel continued. "Tom wanted to take care of her right away, but I've been saving her."

"Saving her? Is that supposed to mean something?" Mary shook her head. "You're doing this somehow." She remembered then how Daniel had looked in the classroom the day before. His closed eyes. "You did it in English, too, didn't you? You made me think I saw that teacher. What are you trying to do to me?" Her voice had risen into a shrill yelp. She had to get out of there.

Mary half-ran down the row of chairs, then sprinted out the door, through the lobby, and into the dark. It had started to rain, and her bare arms were immediately slick from the fine mist.

Footsteps followed her, then yells. Mary pushed past people on the sidewalk and then crossed a street without even looking for traffic. A car honked, but she kept running. A few blocks later she ran out of road and jogged down a short flight of moss-covered concrete steps, onto the rocky beach. Even though she had only been running for a few minutes, she gasped for breath.

Mary never believed that girls fainted in real life like they did in the movies. But now there were splotches of light darting on the edge of her vision. She knew that if she didn't sit down, she would fall. Firm hands grabbed her arms and helped her down onto a piece of driftwood.

"Got you." It was a girl's voice.

"Dan, you scared the poor girl right out of the theater." A guy's voice. Mary looked up, squinting through the tiny raindrops. She could just make out the shape of the moon through the clouds. Mary breathed in the damp, salty air so deeply that it felt like her lungs would burst. Then she screamed.

"Stop it!" A slap knocked her head to the side. Mary took another deep, gasping breath, but this time let it out in a ragged sob. Abby stood over her, hand raised.

"You need to get a grip. Calm down."

"You didn't need to do that." Daniel stood beside Abby.

"Someone's gonna hear her."

"She'll be quiet now. She'll listen. Right, Mary?" Daniel sat on the driftwood beside her, but she edged away from him.

"Dan, you've done enough. She doesn't want you here." Tom pulled Daniel off the log and pointed down the beach. "Time-out."

"What? You can't give me a time-out."

"Time-out. Now."

"You heard him." Abby, who was a half-head taller than Daniel, also pointed. "Go." Dan kicked at the gravelly sand, then stomped away.

Mary started laughing, then covered her mouth. She didn't know why she was laughing.

None of this was funny. Not one thing. But she couldn't stop laughing.

Abby crouched next to her. "Sweetie. Are you ready to listen?" Mary didn't really answer but kept smothering her laughs with both hands. Abby and Tom sat down on either side of her. After a minute of silence, Tom began picking up rocks and flinging them into the water. The soft splash was almost comforting, and Mary was suddenly exhausted.

After a few minutes, Abby stood up. "Okay. Better?" In the dark, it was hard to see Abby's features or the bright color of her hair. She looked so tall, like a statue.

Mary nodded, though she didn't know what *better* could possibly mean in this situation. She wasn't laughing to herself and she wasn't sobbing. That was an improvement. In the distance, she could see the dark shape of Daniel pacing back and forth on the beach.

Tom stepped forward. "There are three things you need to know, and then you can ask questions. Any questions?"

"Tom," Abby said in a low warning voice.

"Sorry. Joke. Anyway, three things. Number one," he held up his pointer finger. "There are ghosts. Yeah . . . that's kind of a big one. Number two, not everyone can see ghosts. You can, obviously—you are a Seer. Number three," he tapped a third finger. "We are Seers too. We get rid of ghosts."

"We're not Ghostbusters," Abby added, and this time Tom shushed her. "I'm just saying, we don't have a ghost-mobile or those ectoplasm things. This isn't like some movie."

"Not a movie. Got it," Mary said, a bit surprised that her voice was steady. She didn't feel very steady.

Tom then made a sweeping gesture with both his hands, much like a ringmaster at a circus. "Any questions?" He should have been wearing a top hat and a shiny vest.

Mary snorted. "Are you serious?" The cool, familiar wind whipped her hair against her face. After growing up in Hawthorne Harbor, the dark, gravelly beaches had become the landscape of her life. Sitting beside the water, with the town at her back, her head cleared and she began to feel stronger. She stood up.

Tom made a slight movement toward her, but Abby once again shook her head at him. He stepped back. "Is that your first question?" He laughed once, almost a seal bark, then began to rub his hands together. "I'm rarely serious. But yes. Right now, I am."

Mary started to walk down the beach, slowly shuffling one foot after the other through the rocks and sand. If she kept walking, she would eventually reach the lighthouse. She could see the pulse of light every few seconds, like a star caught too close to Earth. Before she got to the lighthouse, though, she would reach Daniel. She wanted to talk to him. To hear him explain it.

"Question," she called behind her, as Tom and Abby followed.

"Shoot," Tom answered. He trailed by only a few feet but didn't try to walk beside her.

"Why?"

"Specificity is helpful."

"Why do you get rid of ghosts?"

Daniel was still about twenty feet away and seemed to be digging a hole in the sand with a stick. He probably heard them approaching, but he didn't look up.

Abby answered this one. "Um, because they're ghosts?"

"Casper was a friendly ghost," Tom cut

in. "So Mary might be a tad confused on the subject."

"Ghosts are bad?" Mary asked. "Daniel said the lady in the theater was harmless."

"Really? He said harmless?"

"I never said harmless," Dan called out. He flung his stick out into the waves. "When did I say that?"

Mary groaned in exasperation. "I don't remember exactly what you said. I don't carry around a tape recorder."

"You could use your phone," Tom added. "As a recorder, I mean."

"Not helpful," Abby muttered.

Mary made a noise between a groan and a scoff. "Okay, whatever. This is all nonsense."

"No, you were asking great questions," Tom said. "Gold star. Keep going."

"Okay," Mary said. "If that woman in the theater was a ghost—and I'm not saying she was—then why is she dangerous? She was just watching a movie. And," Mary pointed to Daniel, "you left her there."

"Yeah, well," Daniel looked to Tom. "She is harmless."

"See," Mary said, feeling as though she had proved a point. She just didn't know what that point was yet.

"Dan," Abby began, but Dan interrupted her. "What's she gonna do? Steal popcorn? I'll take care of it later."

"Hey," Tom raised his voice. "Guys, let's stop confusing Mary."

"Yeah, because that is the confusing part," Mary said. The whole night still felt unreal, like she was going to float away if she didn't keep looking down at her feet.

When she was just a few feet from Daniel, Mary stopped. She folded her arms across her chest. Goose bumps rose on her skin and her teeth started to chatter. She was so cold.

"Here," Abby said, draping her coat over Mary's shoulders. "You're freezing."

"Thank you," Mary said. The coat was thin, and the sleeves were way too long, but it was better than nothing in the light rain. Tom collected driftwood to build a fire.

Mary held her hands out in front of the small fire. She was pretty sure they were not supposed to light fires on the beach, and she kept expecting a cop to come by and scold them or write them a ticket.

As flames gnawed on broken pieces of damp driftwood, Mary once again thought of the teacher. Dan had seen Mr. Benson burning too. "So, you hunt ghosts?" she asked them, more casually than she had expected.

Tom answered her. "Yes. Exactly. Sort of. We go where we think there might be ghosts."

"Then you get rid of them?"

"Yep. Can't just leave them hanging around. They get into all kinds of mischief."

"Mischief? What does that mean?"

Abby rolled up her sleeve. In the flickering light of the fire, Mary could just make out a long scar that snaked up her arm. "This kind of mischief."

"A ghost did that?" Mary felt foolish actually saying the word *ghost*. Part of her still suspected that at any moment the three of them were going to start laughing at her. *We fooled you!*

"Ghosts. Two of them, in New Mexico. One held me down and the other tried to carve something into my arm."

"Show-off," Tom said, poking at the fire with a stick.

"They aren't all that bad," Dan added. Abby made a snorting sound.

Silence followed as everyone watched the

fire and listened to the sound of the waves. Mary tried to think of another question to ask, but her questions were too big to put into words. She still didn't quite want to admit that she believed them.

Finally, she said, "How old are you? Are you really in high school?" Dan answered, "Yeah. We're real, live high schoolers. We just move around a lot. The schools think we're army brats. I'm seventeen."

"A gentleman never reveals his age," Tom said.

Abby pointed at Tom. "My brother and I just turned eighteen a few months ago. We're actually adults, if you can believe it." Tom stuck his tongue out at her.

"So, your parents are in the military?"

"No. That's just what we tell the schools," Dan said. Abby gave Dan a stern look before he added, "Parents aren't really a factor."

"You have no parents? Where do you live?"

Tom laughed. "We tell you about ghosts and all you want to know about is if Mommy and Daddy tuck us in at night? Do you want to know my favorite color and if I like long walks on the beach, too?"

"Blue," Abby said, then shoved Tom's shoulder. "And for the record, he loves long walks on the beach."

Mary picked up a smooth rock and passed it back and forth between her hands. "So, we can see ghosts, but most people can't? Why not?"

Abby winked at Mary. "Well, you know why you can see ghosts, right?"

Mary shook her head. "Because this was all a dream?"

"You're in a time warp," Abby said.

Mary glanced at Dan, then looked away. She hoped it was too dark for them to see her eyes roll.

"Abby, grow up." Daniel tossed a twig into the fire.

"Sorry! You all just looked so serious." Abby ran one hand through her long hair, then twisted it over her shoulder like a rope.

Dan broke another twig. "Well it is serious. We're not here to goof off and play high school."

Tom just kept looking back and forth between them like he was watching a TV show. Mary sighed, loudly, but no one seemed to notice.

Abby gestured toward the fire. "Am I playing? Was I playing last month when that ghost tried to rip out your throat and I stopped him? Was I playing in Texas when you almost got us all killed because you weren't prepared? You're not the only one who takes this seriously."

Tom tried to say something, but Abby cut him off with a chop of her arm. "No. You don't get to take his side again. You know what I'm talking about."

Abby turned back to Dan. "You're the one

who thinks this is a game. You want to save them." She laughed, loud and sharp—just like her brother's laugh. "You probably thought you were saving her, too."

She looked at Mary. "I'm sorry. He never should've brought you into this. It was selfish." Abby punctuated the last word by standing up. Mary watched as she walked away. It was only after Abby had disappeared from sight that Mary remembered she was still wearing Abby's coat.

"Sorry about that," Tom said, poking at the fire with a longer stick. "My sister has a bit of a temper."

Dan was perfectly still. His hands were folded in his lap. "She doesn't just have a temper, Tom. She doesn't think. She just does whatever she wants. She's going to get someone killed."

"Guys?" Mary asked. They both turned to

her, their eyes widening slightly as though just realizing she was still there. "I just want to know why I can see ghosts!"

It was Dan who finally answered her. "You are a Seer because your brother died and it changed your brain."

"I'm sorry," Tom said. He held up the burning stick and drew something in the air with the smoke. Mary got up and left.

The porch light was still on when she got home. Moths fluttered around her hair as she unlocked the door. One followed her inside, and she tried to catch it but missed. Her cat, Jack, would probably eat it.

"Good movie?" Mary's dad sat at the kitchen table, phone in both hands. He looked up as she walked into the room.

"Yeah. But I don't think you'd like it." Mary was starving. She grabbed a slice of bread from the bag on the counter, wadded it up in

her hand, and shoved it in her mouth. She did this without thinking—a childhood habit.

"Hungry?" Her dad's gaze slid back to his phone. He was probably playing Candy Crush. He did that when he couldn't sleep.

"A bit."

"Your mom made lasagna. It's in the fridge."

"'Kay," she said, but she just reached for a second slice of bread.

For that first week after Paul's accident, when there was still hope, Mary had never felt closer to her dad. They suddenly had a shared language. How was Paul doing? Had he moved his hand? Did he blink? Could he hear them?

Her father said the accident could have been worse. If Paul had been going a little faster, the engine might have come through the dashboard and crushed him. If he hadn't been wearing his seat belt, he might have gone through the windshield. It was as though they could keep him alive by speaking aloud all of the ways he didn't die. They didn't talk about his missing arm. They didn't talk about how he might never see again.

When her mom brought up plastic surgery, Mary felt her tongue stick to the roof of her mouth like glue. She didn't want to think about what would come after: how her brother would not be her brother anymore, but her brother who had crashed his car. The brother who had ruined his life.

Then after Paul died, it was like she and her dad were refugees from a country they never wanted to talk about again.

"Going to bed?" her dad asked, his eyes back on his phone.

"Yeah."

"'Night, sweetheart."

"'Night."

Mary had to walk past Paul's closed door to reach her room. At first it had seemed like he might still in there. Not anymore. It had been three weeks since he died, and now it felt like a painted door—a scene from that roadrunner cartoon. The roadrunner can walk through the door in the side of a cliff, but when the coyote tries it, it's no longer a real door—just a painting of a door. Mary hated being the coyote.

It wasn't really that late. She picked up her phone and almost pressed James's number before she realized what she was doing. Everything Dan, Tom, and Abby had told her filled her head, the information spinning inside of her brain.

After Abby had stormed off, Tom and Daniel told Mary more about ghosts. Only a few people could see them, but not all Seers saw ghosts the same way. To some, they looked alive. Others saw ghosts as shadows or could only feel them as a cold spot in the room. Usually, the ability surfaced after a traumatic loss.

The three of them traveled around the country, searching for ghosts. They rarely stayed in one place longer than a few months. Mary couldn't imagine not having her room and her cat and her parents. Mary didn't even know if they had parents. Or, if they did, if their parents even knew where they were. Mary didn't even know if Dan, Tom, and Abby were their real names.

Thinking back, Mary realized she still knew pretty much nothing about them. She wasn't even sure why ghosts were dangerous. She didn't know exactly how they "got rid of" the ghosts. They never explained Abby's comment about Texas. Sitting in her room,

Mary knew she needed to talk to someone.

"How'd it go?" Chloe rarely said hello, but just dove right into the conversation. "Did your hands meet in the buttery popcorn?"

"Um, not exactly."

Chloe always made her smile, even when Mary thought that wasn't possible. When Chloe heard that Paul didn't make it, she came right over and talked nonstop about absolutely nothing.

"Did you at least get to first base?" Chloe teased.

"What does that even mean?"

"Kissing. On the mouth."

"Did I kiss Daniel in the movie theater? Is that what you're asking?" Mary turned on her laptop and waited for it to load. She needed a new computer. Hers had been a gift from "Santa" about five years ago, and it couldn't even stream Netflix without crashing.

"Yes. That's exactly what I'm asking."

The computer made a weird grinding sound. "Yes. Right there in front of all the old people and ushers."

"Yes! Hey, I gotta go. The mother is making me watch my sister while she goes out."

"Bye."

"See ya tomorrow."

Mary typed in the keywords: Hawthorne Harbor, Washington, Opal, movie theater, murder. Nothing useful. Hawthorne Harbor, Washington, movie theater, suicide. She had to scroll through three pages before she found it.

Mara Amare, the daughter of Italian immigrants, was found dead in the Opal two days before Christmas, 1916. An apparent suicide. A single gunshot to the head. There was a picture: the same arching eyebrows and dark lips that made her look like she had stepped out of a black-and-white movie. Mara had wanted to be an actress.

There was just one small paragraph about her. Nothing that could tell Mary about the kind of life she had lived or why she would have taken her own life. All that was lost to time.

Mary put away her computer. She lay on the bed and closed her eyes, trying to decide whether today had really happened. She thought about school the next day and wondered what was going to happen next.